ZOO ANIMAL FRIENDS

GORILLAS

AMY CULLIFORD

A Crabtree Roots Book

Crabtree Publishing

crabtreebooks.com

School-to-Home Support for Caregivers and Teachers

This book helps children grow by letting them practice reading. Here are a few guiding questions to help the reader with building his or her comprehension skills. Possible answers appear here in red.

Before Reading:

- What do I think this book is about?
  - *I think this book is about gorillas.*
  - *I think this book is about what gorillas do.*

- What do I want to learn about this topic?
  - *I want to learn where gorillas live.*
  - *I want to learn what colors a gorilla can be.*

During Reading:

- I wonder why...
  - *I wonder why gorillas are black or brown.*
  - *I wonder why gorillas live in forests.*

- What have I learned so far?
  - *I have learned that gorillas like to play.*
  - *I have learned that gorillas can be different colors.*

After Reading:

- What details did I learn about this topic?
  - *I have learned that gorillas eat fruit.*
  - *I have learned that gorillas live in forests.*

- Read the book again and look for the vocabulary words.
  - *I see the word **gorilla** on page 3 and the word **forest** on page 4. The other vocabulary word is found on page 14.*

This is a **gorilla**.

This gorilla is in a **forest**.

Most gorillas are black.

Some gorillas like to play.

All gorillas can run.

All gorillas eat **fruit**.

Word List

Sight Words

a	in	run
all	is	some
are	like	this
can	most	to
eat	play	

Words to Know

forest   **fruit**   **gorilla**

27 Words

This is a **gorilla**.

This gorilla is in a **forest**.

Most gorillas are black.

Some gorillas like to play.

All gorillas can run.

All gorillas eat **fruit**.

Written by: Amy Culliford

Designed by: Rhea Wallace

Series Development : James Earley

Proofreader: Janine Deschenes

Educational Consultant: Marie Lemke M.Ed.

Photographs:
Shutterstock: svetjekolem: cover; Edwin Butter: p. 1, 9; Musicheart7: p. 3, 14; Gudkov Andrey: p. 5, 14; Travel Faery: p. 7; Michael Verbeek: p. 11; Stayer: p. 12, 14

ZOO ANIMAL FRIENDS

GORILLAS

Crabtree Publishing

crabtreebooks.com   800-387-7650

Printed in China/082022/FE052422CT

Published in Canada
Crabtree Publishing
616 Welland Ave.
St. Catharines, Ontario
L2M 5V6

Published in the United States
Crabtree Publishing
347 Fifth Ave
Suite 1402-145
New York, NY 10016

Hardcover	978-1-4271-6035-5
Paperback	978-1-4271-6041-6
Ebook (pdf)	978-1-4271-3327-4
Epub	978-1-4271-3387-8
Read-along	978-1-4271-6059-1
Audio book	978-1-4271-6065-2

Library and Archives Canada Cataloguing in Publication

Title: Gorillas / Amy Culliford.
Names: Culliford, Amy, 1992- author.
Description: Series statement: Zoo animal friends | "A Crabtree rootsbook".
Identifiers: Canadiana (print) 20210177772 | Canadiana (ebook) 20210177780 | ISBN 9781427160355 (hardcover) | ISBN 9781427160416 (softcover) | ISBN 9781427133274 (HTML) | ISBN 9781427133878 (EPUB) | ISBN 9781427160591 (read-along ebook)
Subjects: LCSH: Gorilla—Juvenile literature.
Classification: LCC QL737.P94 C85 2022 | DDC j599.884—dc23

Library of Congress Cataloging-in-Publication Data

Names: Culliford, Amy, 1992- author.
Title: Gorillas / Amy Culliford.
Description: New York : Crabtree Publishing, [2022] | Series: Zoo animal friends - a Crabtree roots book | Includes index. | Audience: Ages 4-6 | Audience: Grades K-1
Identifiers: LCCN 2021014531 (print) | LCCN 2021014532 (ebook) | ISBN 9781427160355 (hardcover) | ISBN 9781427160416 (paperback) | ISBN 9781427133274 (ebook) | ISBN 9781427133878 (epub) | ISBN 9781427160591
Subjects: LCSH: Gorilla--Juvenile literature. | Zoo animals--Juvenile literature.
Classification: LCC SF408.6.A64 C85 2022 (print) | LCC SF408.6.A64 (ebook) | DDC 599.884--dc23
LC record available at https://lccn.loc.gov/2021014531
LC ebook record available at https://lccn.loc.gov/2021014532